Fergus Barnaby lived on the
first floor with Mom and Dad.

It was a very exciting
day because ...

... Fergus Barnaby was
going on **vacation**.

Mom and Dad were busy
packing for the trip.

"Ready yet, Fergus?" asked Dad.
"Don't forget anything!"

"I've packed my suitcase," puffed
Fergus, "and—oh, no …

... my bucket and shovel!
I lent them to Fred
when we were
building a fort."

Fergus Barnaby
climbed up to the
second floor
where Fred lived.

"Hello, Fergus Barnaby."

"Hello, Fred. I'm going on vacation. Can I have my bucket and shovel?"

"Of course, here you go. Send me a photo of your best castle."

Fergus Barnaby

climbed all

the way

down from

the **second** floor

where Fred lived ...

... to the

first floor

where he lived

with Mom and Dad.

He packed his bucket and shovel.

"What else have you forgotten?" asked Dad. He was starting to load up the car.

"Oh, no," said Fergus Barnaby. "My swimming goggles! I lent them to Emily Rose."

He climbed up to the **third** floor where Emily Rose lived.

"Hello, Fergus Barnaby."

"Hello, Emily Rose. Can I have my swimming goggles? I'm going on vacation."

"Sure thing, here you go. Practice for when we go to swimming lessons together."

This is to certify that
EMILY ROSE
has achieved
SILVER
SWIMMING AWARD

Fergus Barnaby climbed
all the way
down
down
from the **third** floor ...

... to the **first** floor where
he lived with Mom and Dad.

... past the **second** floor where Fred lived who had borrowed his bucket and shovel ...

He packed his
swimming goggles.

"Is there anything else you've forgotten?" asked Dad, checking the car.

"Oh, **no**," said Fergus Barnaby. "My kite! I lent it to Teddy when we were playing."

He climbed to the **fourth** floor where Teddy lived.

"Hello, Fergus Barnaby."

"Hello, Teddy. Can I have my kite?"

"No problem, here you go. Have fun."

Fergus Barnaby climbed all the way
down
down
down from the
fourth floor ...

... past the **second** floor where
Fred lived who had borrowed his
bucket and shovel ...

... past the **third** floor where Emily Rose lived who had borrowed his swimming goggles ...

... to the **first** floor where he lived with Mom and Dad.

Fergus Barnaby packed his kite.
"Are you ready now?" asked Dad.

"Oh, YES," said Fergus Barnaby.
"I think I am!"

And so they set
off on vacation.

"OH, NO!" said
Fergus Barnaby ...

"Fergus Barnaby!" said Dad.

"You went **up** to the **fourth** floor to get **your** kite from Teddy.

You went **up** to the **third** floor to get **your** swimming goggles from Emily Rose.

You went **up** to the **second** floor to get **your** bucket and shovel from Fred.

You packed your suitcase on the **first** floor where we live.

What could you possibly have forgotten?"

"WE FORGOT **MOM!**"